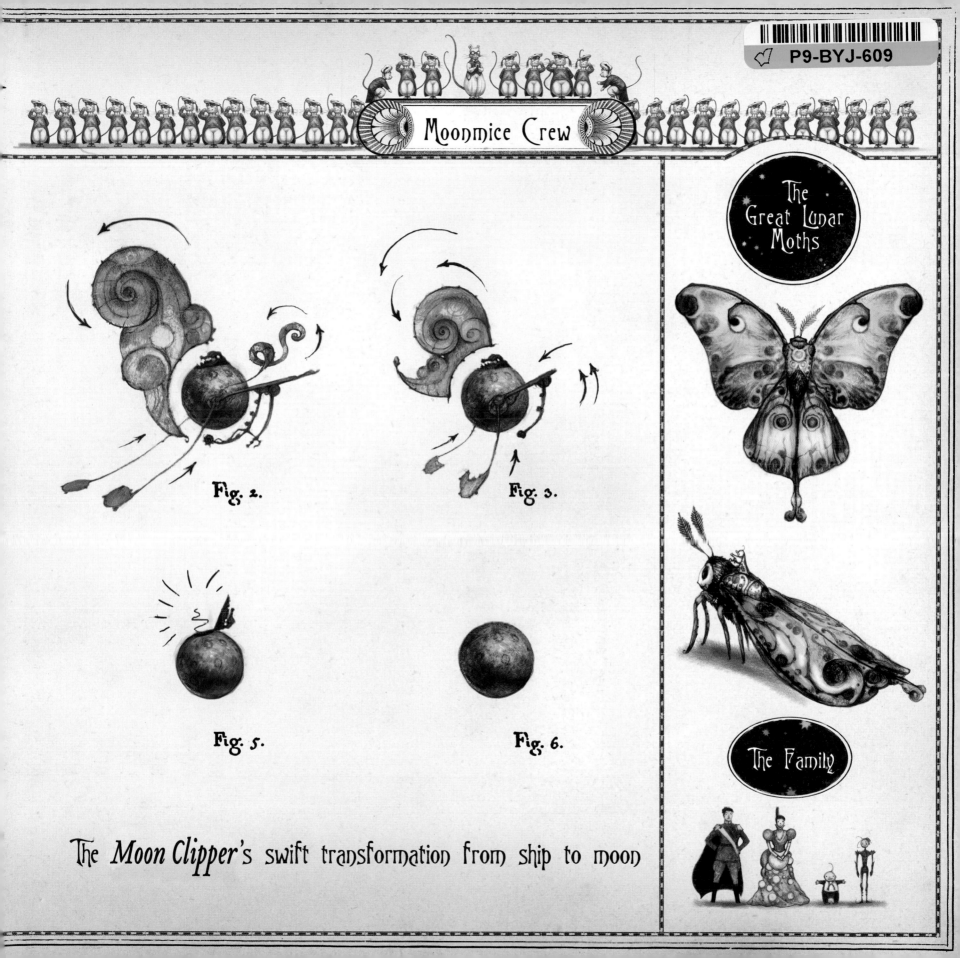

Moonmice Crew

The Great Lunar Moths

The Family

Fig. 2.

Fig. 3.

Fig. 5.

Fig. 6.

The *Moon Clipper's* swift transformation from ship to moon

The Man in the Moon

WILLIAM JOYCE

Edited by Laura Geringer Books

Atheneum Books for Young Readers

New York London Toronto Sydney

Of course you know the Guardians of Childhood.

You've known them since before you can remember and you'll know them till your memories are like twilight: Santa Claus, the Tooth Fairy, the Sandman, the Easter Bunny, and the others. But the very first one was the Man in the Moon.

Many once upon a times ago, the Man in the Moon began his journey. It was during the Golden Age—a glorious time of hope and happiness and dreams that could come true.

As a baby, the Man in the Moon had everything a child could need. His father showed him the wonders of the heavens through his telescope while the Moonbot crew whistled a jolly "Toot toot" to every passing ship. By the light of the giant Glowworms, his mother read to him from her *Primer of Planets* as the Moonmice hushed one another so they could listen too. And he had a devoted little friend named Nightlight to watch over him. Together they all sailed from one peaceful planet to another in their beautiful ship, the *Moon Clipper*.

At night, the *Moon Clipper* was designed to turn into a moon, so Nightlight called the baby the little Man in the Moon—or MiM, for short.

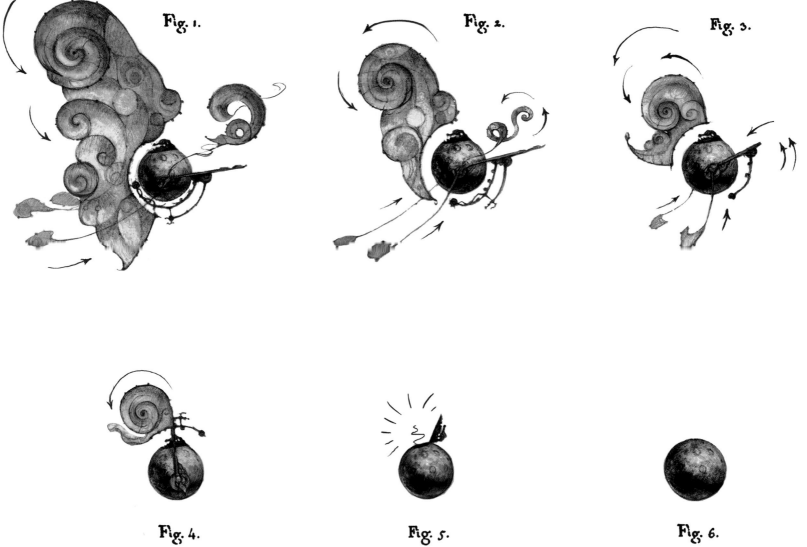

Fig. 1.   Fig. 2.   Fig. 3.

Fig. 4.   Fig. 5.   Fig. 6.

Nightlight never slept, and every night he sprinkled Dreamsand over MiM and sang him a lullaby:

"Nightlight, bright light,
Sweet dreams I bestow.
Sleep tight, all night.
Forever I will glow."

And as long as Nightlight watched over him, MiM was safe from nightmares.

But darkness came to the Golden Age. It came in the shifting shape of Pitch, the King of Nightmares. He had heard of the boy who had never had a nightmare. And this he could not abide. So he vowed to make that boy his own—a Prince of Nightmares. In search of MiM, Pitch sailed in his *Nightmare Galleon* on waves of fear—plundering planets, extinguishing stars, and scuttling every airship that crossed his path.

MiM's parents knew of the perfect place to hide—an unchartered little green and blue planet in a distant galaxy. It was called Earth, and it had no moon. The *Moon Clipper* glided in deepest silence, speeding away from Pitch's darkness.

Suddenly, out of the gloom, the *Nightmare Galleon* appeared, so close MiM could see Pitch standing on the bow.

"Toot toot?" asked the baby.

"Where is that oh so innocent child who has never had a nightmare?" Pitch demanded, glaring straight at MiM.

Then he signaled the attack.

MiM's parents commanded Nightlight to take the baby to a hidden nursery deep in the darkest tunnels of the ship.

"But first you must kneel and take this oath," they said. Their voices rang out through the smoldering smoke and flame:

"Watch over our child. Guide him safely from the ways of harm.
Keep happy his heart, brave his soul, and rosy his cheeks.
Guard with your life his hopes and dreams,
For he is all that we have, all that we are,
And all that we will ever be."

The battle rocked the *Moon Clipper* as Nightlight rushed MiM to safety. Seeing a tear on the frightened child's cheek, he took it and held it close to his heart. Fiercely, he repeated his oath. Then he felt a searing pain. When he opened his hand, the tear had changed into a brilliant diamond, sharp as a dagger.

"Remember me in dreams," he whispered to MiM as he flickered away to face Pitch.

The galaxies had never known such a battle. MiM's parents and their crew fought valiantly, but they were overwhelmed at last. MiM's parents were captured, and all seemed lost.

Nightlight knew what he must do. Whatever the cost, MiM must not become a Prince of Nightmares! With the diamond dagger held aloft, Nightlight flew bravely forward. He aimed the weapon at Pitch's heart. There was a blinding flash, then a great explosion!

When all was still, MiM crawled up to the surface.

"Toot? Toot?" he whispered. His parents didn't answer.

He looked around him. Pitch and his galleon had vanished. The beautiful hull of the *Moon Clipper* had been blasted away. It was now just a moon and would never sail again.

"Toot?" he called once more, and listened. Again, no answer came.

Finally, he looked up at the sky.

He saw a group of new stars, shimmering above him. He stared at them until he was sure. His mother and father were there. Far away, but still there.

But what of noble little Nightlight? The baby glimpsed a shooting star, as bright as Dreamsand, as it fell to Earth.

Slowly the remaining Moonbots, Moonmice, and giant Glowworms surrounded MiM. The only words he knew were "Toot toot," so he said them over and over again. Gently they lifted MiM up and carried him into the tunnels of the moon. The baby looked up at the sky and waved, gazing longingly at his parents' constellation.

Now he truly was MiM—the little Man in the Moon.

iM's new life had many comforts. Every night, one of the Lunar Moths would circle the moon with MiM on its soft, woolly back. He'd stay awake long enough to see his parents' constellation. Then he'd sleep and dream of Nightlight and their gentle Golden Age.

As time passed, the moon became a planet-sized playground for the boy. There was so little gravity that with one hop he could bounce over the tallest mountain. After a long day of adventuring, dinners were always a treat!

Lunar Ice Cream! Comet Surprise! Space Juice Nectarine!
And each meal was lit by schools of Starfish that swam
through the evening sky.

As young MiM wandered through the moon's tunnels, he discovered the primer his mother used to read to him. In the book was something he had completely forgotten— the little green and blue planet! He ran to his father's telescope. As he peered into it, he remembered the long-ago shooting star that had fallen to Earth. But it was not Nightlight he found.

"There are children on Earth! Children like me!" he cried.

Years went by, and the Man in the Moon was no longer a little boy.

His new friends on Earth were very far away, but their lost balloons often floated up to the moon. MiM found that if he held them to his ear, he could hear the hopes and dreams of the children who had lost them. He listened carefully. Soon he had a whole collection of lost balloons.

MiM learned that sometimes the children just needed a toy or a candy or a prize or a sweet dream or a good story to cheer them up.

So MiM gazed down upon the Earth, scanning mountaintops so remote, they were hidden in clouds. There he found a grand toy maker to make the children toys, a regal rabbit to make them candy eggs, and a fairy from the kingdom of Punjam Hy Loo to leave prizes under their pillows. He even found a sleepy little fellow on a faraway sandy island who seemed to know all there was to know about dreams. And lastly, MiM brought the children of Earth a lovely lady who would tell them stories.

ut for all the joy MiM brought to Earth, there was one thing he had not been able to change: The children were still afraid of the dark. Although Pitch and his Nightmare Men were nowhere to be seen, MiM knew that the children still had nightmares. And after all this time, he had never had one himself. MiM thought he would know everything when he grew up, but of course he did not. "This growing up is a tricky business," he said to himself. Every day he listened to the lost balloons, and watched the children through his telescope, and wondered how he could help them.

If only I could find them a friend like Nightlight, he thought.

And so, deep in thought and remembering his friend, MiM kicked a rock, and then another, revealing a pile of very bright sand. He stopped and stared. It reminded him of the Dreamsand that Nightlight had sprinkled over him when he was a baby!

MiM laughed to himself and went on kicking rocks. He had an idea.

Soon the Moonbots and Moonmice were kicking rocks too. When the Moonmice were so tired that they could hardly hold up their tails and the Moonbots were so creaky that they could barely move, MiM called upon the toy maker and the rabbit, the fairy and the others from Earth to fly up and lend a hand. And then finally, when everyone was too tired even to complain, the Man in the Moon smiled and summoned the Lunar Moths.

The bright sand had made the moon one hundred times brighter. "Now the children of Earth will see the moon's smiling face and know they have a Nightlight to guard them forever!" said MiM. And for a moment the distant stars of his mother and father sparkled more brightly than ever before. MiM began to sing. It was an old song, a beloved song, and they all joined in:

"Nightlight, bright light,
Sweet dreams I bestow.
Sleep tight, all night.
Forever I will glow."

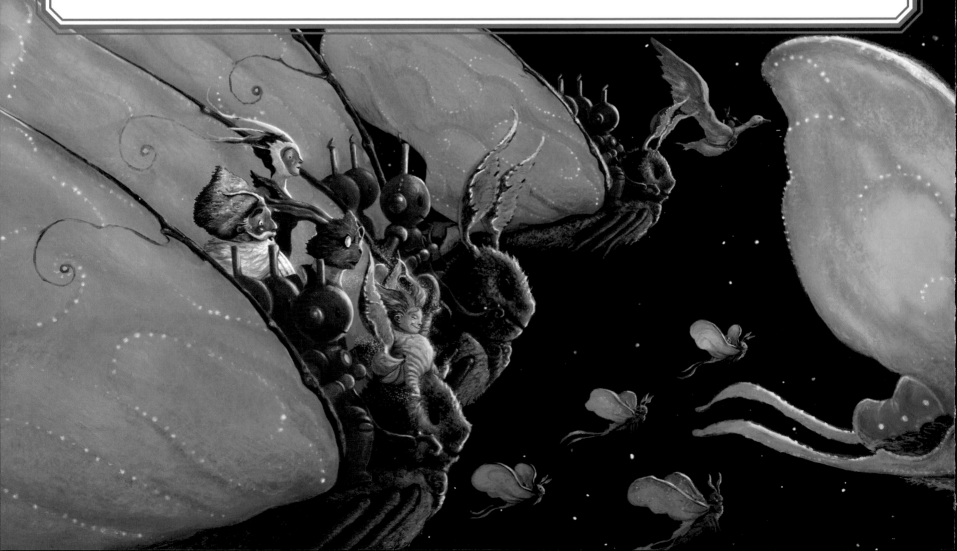

The Man in the Moon knew then that he could be a guardian of the children of Earth, just as Nightlight had been his guardian long ago. But he would need help.

And so he gathered everyone together. "Now my friends," he said, "kneel and take this oath." It was much like the one Nightlight had taken long ago, and now it would be their own:

> *"We will watch over the children of Earth,*
>   *Guide them safely from the ways of harm,*
>   *Keep happy their hearts, brave their souls, and rosy*
>   *their cheeks.*
>   *We will guard with our lives their hopes and dreams,*
>   *For they are all that we have, all that we are,*
>   *And all that we will ever be."*

So began the Guardians of Childhood.

And for the children of Earth, the night was never again as dark.

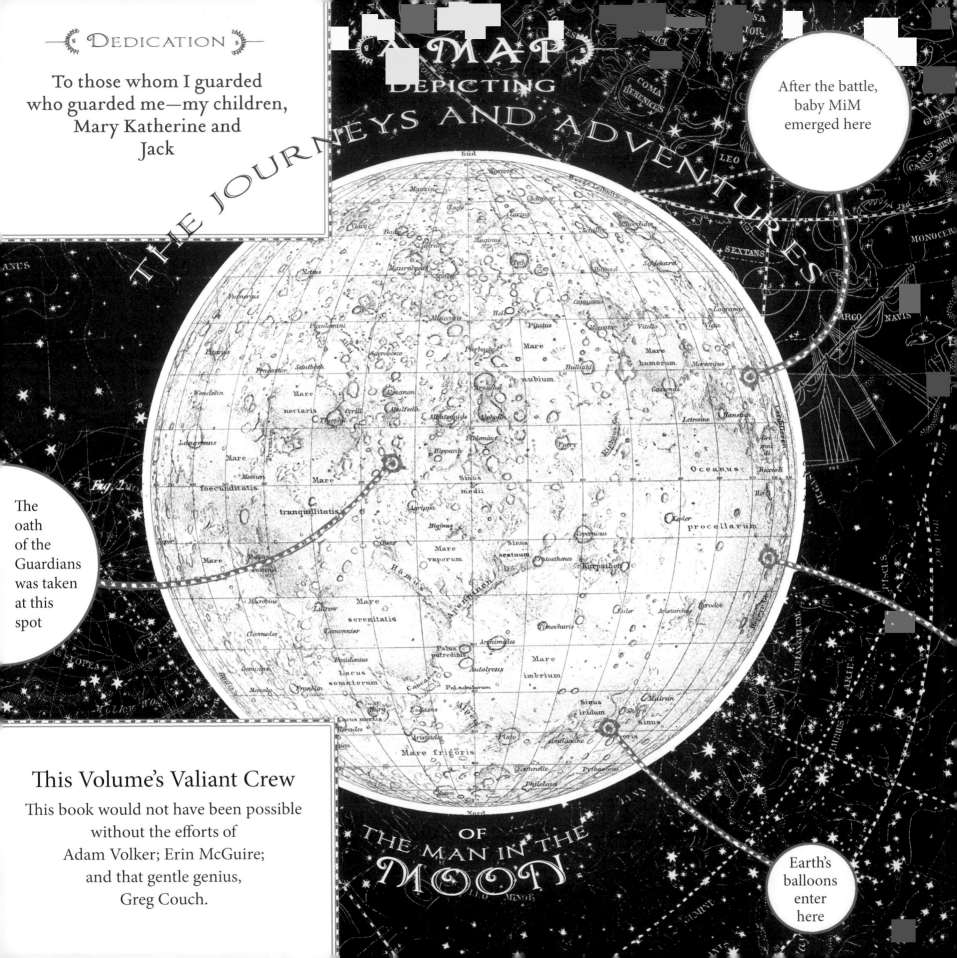

DEDICATION

To those whom I guarded
who guarded me—my children,
Mary Katherine and
Jack

A MAP
DEPICTING
THE JOURNEYS AND ADVENTURES

After the battle,
baby MiM
emerged here

The
oath
of the
Guardians
was taken
at this
spot

The
oath
of the
Guardians
was taken
at this
spot

This Volume's Valiant Crew

This book would not have been possible
without the efforts of
Adam Volker; Erin McGuire;
and that gentle genius,
Greg Couch.

OF
THE MAN IN THE
MOON

Earth's
balloons
enter
here

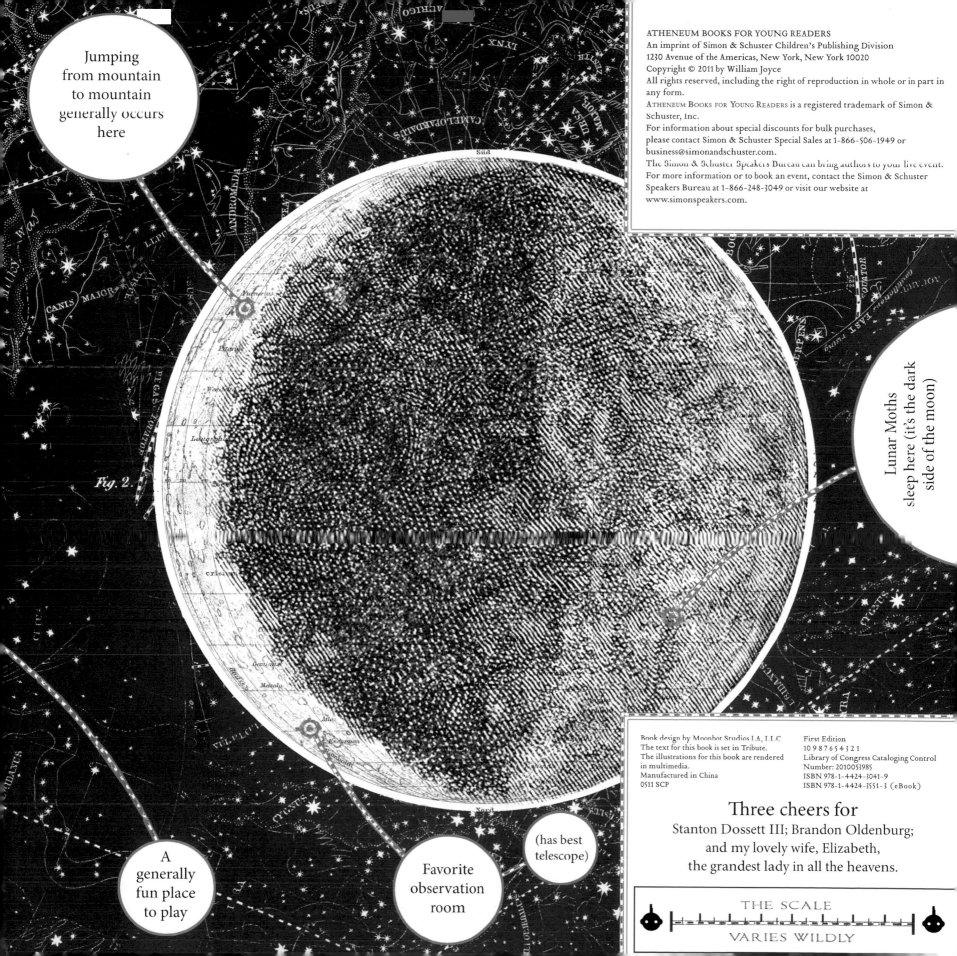

Jumping
from mountain
to mountain
generally occurs
here

Lunar Moths
sleep here (it's the dark
side of the moon)

A
generally
fun place
to play

Favorite
observation
room

(has best
telescope)

ATHENEUM BOOKS FOR YOUNG READERS
An imprint of Simon & Schuster Children's Publishing Division
1230 Avenue of the Americas, New York, New York 10020
Copyright © 2011 by William Joyce
All rights reserved, including the right of reproduction in whole or in part in
any form.
ATHENEUM BOOKS FOR YOUNG READERS is a registered trademark of Simon &
Schuster, Inc.
For information about special discounts for bulk purchases,
please contact Simon & Schuster Special Sales at 1-866-506-1949 or
business@simonandschuster.com.
The Simon & Schuster Speakers Bureau can bring authors to your live event.
For more information or to book an event, contact the Simon & Schuster
Speakers Bureau at 1-866-248-3049 or visit our website at
www.simonspeakers.com.

Book design by Moonbot Studios LA, LLC
The text for this book is set in Tribute.
The illustrations for this book are rendered
in multimedia.
Manufactured in China
0511 SCP

First Edition
10 9 8 7 6 5 4 3 2 1
Library of Congress Cataloging Control
Number: 2010053985
ISBN 978-1-4424-3041-9
ISBN 978-1-4424-3551-3 (eBook)

Three cheers for
Stanton Dossett III; Brandon Oldenburg;
and my lovely wife, Elizabeth,
the grandest lady in all the heavens.

THE SCALE
VARIES WILDLY

The Moon Clipper
at full sail

The most beautiful craft
of the Golden Age

Fig. 1.

Fig. 4.

The
Glow-
worms